The Dream

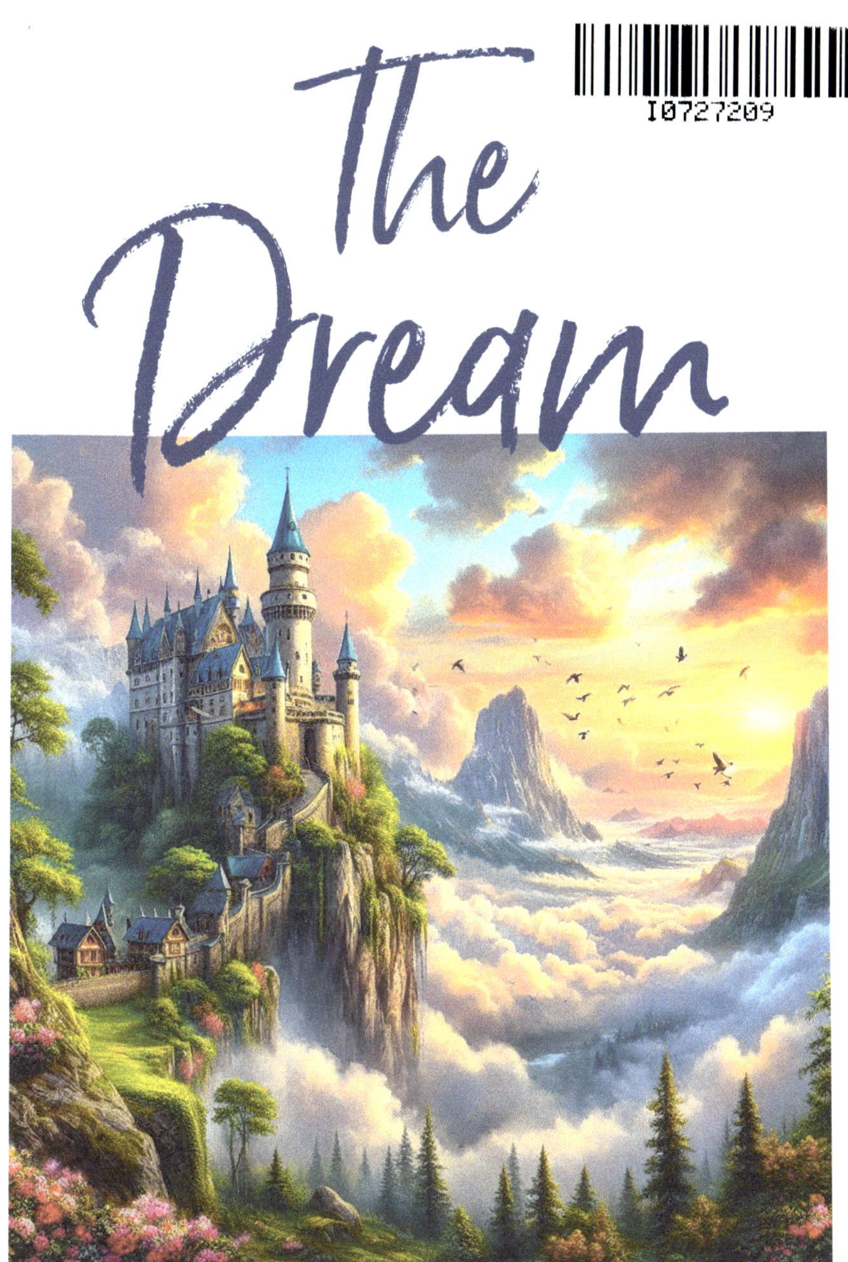

Rox and Charles

Published by

ICABOD Press

ISBN: 978-1-946858-81-8 (Paperback)
ISBN: 978-1-946858-82-5 (eBook)

Library of Congress Control Number: 2024921374
Cover and interior design: F + P Graphic Design, FPGD.com
Illustrations by AI

First Edition
Printed in the United States

YOUNG ADULT FICTION | FANTASY

chapter one

Leaving the city and stepping into the enchanted forest, two young siblings faced the challenge of disappearing unnoticed.

Valerian, cautious by nature, brushed the debris from his dark, wavy hair and dark clothing as he rose from under the thick hedges. "Why must we leave the walled city of Settlefore for the forest? Our elders have warned us not to explore, particularly after the last time." His words carried a weight of caution she'd always ignored.

Destiny stepped confidently over the loose rock even though Valerian braced to catch her a few times. Her baggie, oversized overalls, and brown shirt hid most of her budding feminine charms and their status. She couldn't hide her blond hair, cherubic facial features, and sparkling green eyes that matched her brother's.

Despite the odds, Destiny's charming, romantic optimism shone through. "It's all right, Val. I had another dream. I know it's out here…somewhere. We have to look." Her unwavering determination was infectious, even to the cautious Valerian.

Valerian scrutinized the rutted dirt road sprinkled with rocky gravel that stretched toward the majestic granite mountains in the distance. "I don't know how farmers and ranchers get their produce to the city over this trail. Thankfully, it hasn't rained in a while. I'm not sure why you insist we must journey here."

When she paused and turned, he was silenced by her disdainful look. Then, like a nymph without a care, she bounded ahead with her long, loose braids bouncing to her beat. Valerian, three years older, showed increased muscle and broadening shoulders. A mere two summers until his maturity, he followed closely, staying alert to the surroundings, determined to keep his sister safe. His dark brown hair was usually tied into a short ponytail, keeping the hair out of his eyes. His hooded cape was designed to hide his brooding features and mask his pessimistic outlook.

He broke the long silence after they'd traveled a mile or so. "Tell me about the dream again. Maybe it'll help take my mind off our long journey over this forbidden trail." Valerian studied the narrow path and the steep rocky drop-offs on either side.

Destiny giggled with glee. He knew she enjoyed captivating people with her story-telling, especially recounting her visions. She'd once said dreams were mystical nourishment. She was only nine years old, but her twelve-year-old older brother, Valerian, was the one who took her seriously. "Do you want me to babble as we head into the dark forest to keep you from nervousness or because my dreams usually come true?"

They carefully picked their way over the loose rock, helping steady one another when missteps caused stones to slip over the edge. Valerian confessed, "I get cautious when we go into the forest." Guiding her shoulders, he gently centered her on the path, the forest trees thickening on each side. "But I honestly want to know about these dreams of yours."

He presumed her expression was the funny, glassy-eyed stare she got when she recounted the memories. "He's here. I saw him fall from the sky. His armor is almost like skin, bright and shiny. He'll talk to us, but we won't under-stand. I believe he's looking for something."

Valerian rolled his eyes behind her back while matching her foot placement. "This sounds as bad as when I fell into the river while we were fishing, and you had to help get the carp fish out of my pants once I crawled onto the shore. You said it would happen because you dreamt it. Ugh."

"I wasn't making fun of you. I was trying to warn you about falling in. Having all that bait in your waist bag got all the fish to join you for dinner."

"See?" He complained. "No reasonable person could foresee that type of accident. My adorable sister, you shouldn't be telling people about things that will happen. I heard one parent worry that you would start casting spells and turn individuals into toads."

She snickered, "Some folks around us were toads long before I was born." Destiny froze in mid stride. "Val, off the road now," she hissed. "Someone's coming."

They darted into the underbrush of the forest and stilled their breathing.

A broad-shouldered, heavy-set man with a bow and an arrow notched paused within Valerian's line of sight. His deep voice rumbled, "Keep looking. I'm sure I hit it. A wild pig that size will feed our families for a week."

Moments later, after thrashing around the low scrub foliage looking for tracks and broken branches, the two hunters moved on. Destiny and Valerian quietly waited. Valerian gasped when he spied a large, tusked animal behind him. The raspy sounds of struggling breathing showed in the intermittent rise and fall of its leathery sides.

He nudged Destiny and pointed to the wounded animal. Startled, she recoiled in fear, then quietly exclaimed, "It's Tusker. He's hurt."

As she started to advance, Valerian, worried about her safety, restrained her arm.

She shrugged off his grasp. "The hunter was right. His arrow hit the target."

"Destiny, a three-hundred-pound animal with six-inch tusks, isn't our friend," he whispered as she reached to stroke the beast. "What are you doing? You've heard the stories about this monster. The people hunting him wanted him dead because of the people he's injured. I don't want one of them to be you. Let's go."

"No. It's like in the dream. Valerian, I will get some tree moss to plug the wound, and we'll remove the arrow."

His skin felt clammy as she scampered away to find nature's dressing. The animal grunted. Tempted to run, he sighed with relief when she reappeared with the moss in hand. As she set the moss on the side of the animal, she encouraged

Valerian to rest his palm like hers on the animal's shoulder, to feel the heartbeat.

"He will live if we remove the arrow and plug the wound." She added with a defiant look at her brother, "We can't let another life expire because we're scared."

Heartened, Valerian carefully placed a foot on the back of Tusker and grasped the arrow with both hands. "Ready? On the count of three."

She nodded.

"One, two, three." He pulled hard and the arrowhead cleared the skin. He turned it, inspecting it from all angles. "Good, the end of it came out clean."

Tusker groaned with agony but no ear-splitting squeal. Destiny applied the cooling moss treatment, packing it into the ragged edges of the hole. It seemed to ease Tusker's pain as the creature released a long breath, then loudly inhaled. She looked over her shoulder. "Hope the hunters were too far away to hear us." She patted the poultice firmly to

ensure it wouldn't slip off when the animal moved.

Destiny stroked the animal's muzzle while she stared into his eyes. "Okay, buddy. Do like in my dream. Rest, and let the wound soak up the healing elements. I'll keep the arrow and return it to the hunter, saying we found it but no wild boar. They'll give up for now and return home."

chapter two

"Valerian, give Tusker some water, he's thirsty."

Valerian flinched. "We don't want to waste water at this stage in our journey. We might need it,"

"We're going to find streams as we walk, He needs it more than we do."

Valerian grumbled. "You're insisting we give our water to him and..."

Destiny shook her head and snatched the water pouch strap from his shoulder. She bent to pour the life-giving liquid into his open jaws. Tusker gulped down the water, leaving them with only one swallow each.

Tusker laid his head back and grunted with one eye on his savior.

Destiny smiled and patted his snout. "You're welcome."

Valerian, confused, snapped his head,

looking between his sister and the animal. "Who are you talking to?"

"Tusker, of course. Didn't you hear him say thanks?"

Annoyed, Valerian snapped, "I heard this four-legged sponge moan after you gave it all our water."

Her eyes widened. "Wow. Only I can understand what he's saying. Interesting."

"Great. In addition to your bizarre dreams, you understand animal speak, which you failed to mention. We probably shouldn't return to Cloud City. They'll think you're evil or that I'm a nut case for escorting you."

Twirling the arrow absentmindedly with her fingers, Destiny protested. "I am not evil. I know how to do stuff others don't."

"True that." He rose and brushed off his clothing, worrying what else she'd not shared about her dream. "Let's move on to fulfill your dream. We'll see if we can find some water to refill the bladder."

They hadn't traveled far when they jumped at the sound of the booming voice. "Why are you so far from the city?" demanded the hunter.

Afraid she'd answer with whimsey. Valerian blurted, "We were looking for truffles but stumbled, spilling all our water. We are searching for a stream or pond."

The hunter pointed to Destiny. "Where did you get my arrow?"

"Your arrow? I always get yelled at if I leave my toys out rather than put them away," she said with twinkling eyes. "Where did you leave it last?"

"I was hunting an old wild pig. I'm sure I hit him with my arrow. How did you come by it?"

Destiny casually swirled the item. "We found it lying on the path and picked it up. It looks useful."

"That means I didn't hit him after all." The hunter shook his head, looking sad. He wiggled his fingers. "I want my arrow back."

In a teasing mood, Destiny retorted, "I want it as a souvenir for our adventure. I won't tell anyone that you missed your target."

Worried that the hunter would pull another arrow from his quiver and insist, Valerian seized the arrow and pitched it to the man. "Sorry, mister. We hope you have better luck next time."

Angrily, the hunter slid the arrow into his quiver. After several minutes of staring at the young'uns, he left, calling to his friend.

chapter three

Destiny gracefully bounded toward the unknown as if dancing on air, oblivious to the rocks, sticks, and crater-ridden dirt on the zigzag path woven through the darkening forest. Her brother groaned at every other step where he stumbled and tripped, unable to negotiate a smooth advancement.

I don't like this," he whined. "If I'm destined to trip over everything, I'll stay on all fours and pray not to go face down."

Destiny stopped. "Did you hear that? Something's right behind us, Val. We need to run."

"I'm going as fast as I can. I don't know how

you delicately pick your way on this miserable footpath.”

“Pick up your feet,” Destiny challenged.

"Pretend you're dancing the high step with that pretty redhead who makes you tongue-tied. Knees up. Now run."

And they did. They continued nonstop for twenty minutes before they paused, gasping for air. They heard the sound of a pursuer gaining ground. Exchanging alarmed looks, they raced off terrified. Fear drove them until Valerian's legs cramped, forcing him to stop and lean against a tree, silently begging for relief.

"Destiny, I can't go any further. Keep going. I'll stay and buy you time to hide." He grabbed a sturdy staff from the side of the trail and turned to protect his sister from the unknown. "Go now."

Torn between running to hide and remaining with her brother, Destiny hesitated. Seconds later, a massive figure burst into the small clearing to face them. "Tusker," she exclaimed in between deep inhales.

Valerian positioned himself in the path, raising his defensive weapon. The beast grunted and snorted, its sides heaving.

"We didn't know it was you," she declared before she rushed toward him and threw her arms around his neck. She paused and checked his wound.

Clucking his tongue, Valerian wandered next to Tusker, who promptly relieved himself, splattering onto the young man's shoes. The animal snorted and grunted, clearly offering commentary.

Destiny giggled at her brother's expression and translated, "He says that because we were so kind to share our water, he's sharing his water with us."

Valerian shook his shoe to clear off the mess and turned his head from side to side in disbelief. "Charmed, I'm sure." Clearing his throat, he added, "Since you're chatting with this inarticulate and mannerless beast, ask if he knows of any freshwater streams. We need to fill our water bladders and wash my shoes."

chapter four

Destiny and Valerian flinched while ducking when a large black raven swooped in low over their heads, ruffling their hair. It pirouetted then pulled up sharply to gracefully land on Tusker's back. The swine never moved as the claws of the bird touched down.

Valerian was flabbergasted by the sight. "I felt the wind move and heard his feathers crinkle as he landed. How about you, Sis?"

She nodded agreement, then tilted her head toward the loud caws from the visitor. Destiny grinned. "Nice to meet you, Bran. Welcome to our journey." She grabbed the nearly empty water bag and offered, "You're a beautiful, glossy traveler. Would you like a sip of water? We don't have much but would like to share."

Bran cawed in his throat like a hymn, then hopped onto Tusker's head. He leaned toward the girl and clucked.

Destiny opened the bag. "Good idea. Any drops that escape will land on Tusker."

Valerian stomped his feet, incensed. "This is crazy, Destiny! You're acting delusional, thinking you can talk to birds and pigs. You're going too far, squandering away our water."

Unperturbed, she focused intently on the traveler, who bobbed his head and squeaked a few times before taking wing.

She eyed her brother with a smile. "Bran is going to look for food we can eat. He said water is available in a hidden stream within five hundred paces, off to the right. He warned it's too steep for us to go to as we'll get stuck. He told Tusker to use a sturdy vine to lower one of us to fill the water bag. Tusker will do it twice, but the first bag will help him heal."

Valerian mentally counted to ten. "We're taking orders from a crow?"

Tusker bristled and snorted, then looked to his left.

She chuckled. "Tusker said Bran is not a crow but a raven. He insists ravens are noble, but crows are thieves and can't be trusted." She grabbed his hand. "Let's go find water. Maybe Bran will return with directions to food."

Destiny pulled her brother along as she skipped. Tusker followed with his inarticulate grunts.

Valerian dejectedly mumbled, "I wonder when I will wake from this nightmare."

chapter five

The sounds of water navigating the riverbed's rocks echoed up the sheer canyon walls. Valerian inhaled as he peered over the edge and into the clear stream, grateful it was not a raging torrent but a long way down. He located several vines to create a makeshift harness for his sister.

"If you can communicate with Tusker, tell him I will secure it to him, and help lower you. You'll need to face the wall and use your toes to maintain a bit of distance as you go down and return."

Tusker squealed and grunted.

"He understands you," she said with an innocent expression.

"Fine. I don't want to lose you to the river. Even though it is not rushing, I don't know

how to save you. You have to go down because you can't pull me up. Please take care to move slowly."

"I will. It's just like my dream."

He rolled his eyes, secured the harness to Destiny, and wrapped the thick vines around Tusker's foot. He added a braided vine between his sister's waist and the thick vines extending to the bottom.

"Give me both hands."

She complied with a sweet smile.

"I'm going to lift you over the edge. I want you to release one hand, grab the vine, and then the other. I will feed down the length. Tusker will have you if my hands slip."

Sweat beaded on his brow as he tried to squelch the terror in the pit of his stomach during her descent. He breathed a sigh of relief when she reached the water, balancing a toe on a large rock like a fairy on a leaf. Leaning over, she filled the bag and waved. She returned with the bag of water as planned. Tusker immediately consumed the liquid, not wasting a drop.

Val raised his lip and groused, "I would have liked a sip at least."

"I'm ready to go again, Valerian," she announced.

Bran swooped in with a wave of air and chatter as he landed on Tusker's back.

"I understand. I need to go down and retrieve water for us to carry. Tusker finished the first bag full. Please give us a little time." She backstepped to go, but her brother stopped her.

He carefully checked the vines, and one of the lead lengths broke in his hands when he raised it.

Destiny paled to a pasty shade of gray, appearing almost stricken.

Valerian patted her shoulder, hoping to convey reassurance he wasn't convinced of. "Let me cut another that isn't so brittle and rethread it."

She inhaled, visibly calming.

He tied the new thicker vine between Tusker and her vest. She looked at it closely and nodded agreement at the finished knot. She stepped back into the abyss with confidence.

When she returned with the filled bag, Valerian insisted she take the first drink.

Bran incessantly chattered and bobbed his head.

Impatience registered on Destiny's face. She demanded, "Bran, talk slower. I can't understand what you're trying to say." She gave the bird a sip of water, which helped him calm enough to slow his squawks.

Destiny's eyes widened as the chatter from the bird continued. She grabbed Tusker and faced her brother. "We must hurry to the forest's edge to speak with him."

"Uh, I've seen this show before," he grumbled, "It's where one player gets whacked with a stick. I see that look in your eye. What's up?"

Ignoring the question, Destiny grabbed the water and rushed after Bran with Tusker on her heels.

Valerian pouted. "She's got the water, so I must follow." He rushed in the right direction only to stumble a few times. He paused and sucked in gulps of air. "I guess I need to use the dance steps she taught me to avoid falling."

He reached them in time to see Bran soar to the top of a tree, guessing this provided a commanding view.

Destiny and Tusker were at the edge of a vast meadow when he caught up to the troop. Bran perched at the center top of the tree.

Destiny surveyed the area. "Where is he?" she asked, looking at the raven.

Bran bobbed and cawed.

"What do you mean, I need to ask for a favor? We're at the edge of a meadow next to you, a tree, and a giant boulder. What guardian are you talking..."

A loud grinding sound filled the air while the giant boulder appeared to come alive with rough edges rising. A massive spined head with golden eyes faced the girl. Warm air escaped from what could only be nostrils. Interlocked scales clapped over the large frame like waves racing to the shore.

Valerian, frozen in his tracks, felt the warmth of Tusker at his side. The boar squealed, sounding scared. The raven lit gently on Destiny's shoulder.

Destiny whispered, "This is the guardian?"

Bran bobbed and softly cawed.

33

Valerian watched as the dragon pressed his head as close to the ground as possible, with tones and whistles filling the air.

Destiny said, "He stated he's the guardian of this realm. Bran told him to help the one known as Dreamer."

Valerian held onto his sanity by a thread, hoping to protect his sister, though he was frozen to the spot. He scanned the massive creature from tail to nose, searching for wings he'd heard about from stories.

Destiny continued, "The guardian also said, and her brother too."

chapter six

Destiny stared at the enormous creature, trying to see the honor of its soul. "You are big but not fearsome. I am called Destiny, my brother is Valerian, and Tusker is our friend. Bran, the raven, you know. What is your name?"

"Long ago, I was called Soarant."

"Nice to meet you, Soarant. Will you be the guardian champion who will carry us across the savannah? Bran told me of your kind heart, trustworthiness, and heroic endeavors."

The dragon snorted toward his side. "I cannot take you. I promised I'd wait for her. You must not ask me to leave without her."

"We would not have you betray a trust or your word," she agreed. "Walking, rather than flying with you, would take us weeks. We don't have provisions for that long of a journey."

Destiny released a sigh of relief and a slight curve of her lips as understanding registered on her brother's face.

He said, "For whom do you wait, Soarant, mighty creature? Another dragon?"

A wistful grumble left Soarant's massive throat as he shook his enormous horned head. "No, young one. Her name is Butterfly. She is the most delicate and beautiful flying creature I've ever seen. She came from the savannah, and we became friends. I was happy with her by my side. One day, she said she had to return. I, of course, promised to fly her any-where. She bid me to wait for her return. Thus, I am promised to wait."

Valerian pulled Destiny to his side. "My darling sister, dragons reportedly live for many years. He is foolishly waiting for a butterfly that lives weeks at best. We're trapped."

Destiny smiled and motioned for Bran to join a huddle with her, Valerian, and Tusker. Once they were gathered close, she related a possible solution.

After a few minutes, Tusker snorted and grunted enthusiastically. In approval, Bran bobbed his ebony head and promptly took wing into the savannah's warm sunlight.

Valerian grabbed his sister's hand and pulled it toward his heart. "What if the dragon won't accept the offer?"

Destiny sighed. "We need his help. The only way to achieve our goals is with him. Besides, we can't leave Soarant like this, waiting forever. He is a noble, trusting creature who deserves more. We must try." The hours slowly passed. To pass the time, Destiny muttered as if practicing a speech to share with many people.

Late afternoon, Tusker bounded to Destiny and bowed, grunting rapidly. She immediately scanned the horizon.

Her bright eyes sparkled as she spotted the raven in the distance, approaching with a large plant clasped in his beak. He landed gently, setting the delicate foliage on the ground. Using his feet, he quickly clawed a hole in the fertile soil and carefully replanted the treasure.

With chirping and clicking sounds, he asked Destiny to use some of the precious water reserves to nourish it. Destiny smiled at the result as the leaves stretched toward the sky, almost like magic.

She approached the dragon respectfully, diverting his attention from the sky and adding a deep curtsy. "Soarant, I must tell you something awful and then something wonderful. The awful thing will hurt for a moment. For this, I'm sorry. The wonderful thing will make your heart soar. You'll be compelled to take us on our quest when you understand and believe."

Soarant dejectedly shook his massive head, shedding a few scales onto the ground. "My heart is too heavy to let me fly. My friend, Butterfly, is the only one who can allow me to fly again."

Destiny grinned. "I understand. Here is the first part of your next chapter. Your Butterfly had to leave, never to return as you knew her, because of her life cycle. She left you all her children to ensure you will never be alone again. Behold her gift of unending friendship and love to you."

Valerian carefully turned up one leaf after another to show the delicate eggs lying and maturing. He pointed to some caterpillars moving busily on the plant. "These are small lives you will recognize soon."

Destiny raised her hand and stroked the cheek of the mammoth creature. "Butterfly knew she couldn't live as long as you, so she laid the eggs of her children to be with you forever. You need to gather more of these plants and bring them here to give these young creatures enough food to grow into butterflies. They will all be your friends. Please take us across the savannah. We will help find more of these plants for your gentle-winged family."

Tears rolled down his scale-covered cheek. As they slowly worked its way down its face, he commanded, "Catch a tear with your finger and smear it across your forehead. It will ensure good fortune and luck on your travels. You have indeed given me something that fills my heart with hope. At first dawn, I will take you and your companions across the savannah."

chapter seven

At first light, the rustle of Bran's wings awak-
ened Destiny. He landed onto a rock, spun

around, and then chattered excitedly while bobbing his head. She studied the bird's movements and sighed when Tusker joined her.

The fear of failure pricked her heart, as she drew deep breaths. "Tusker, can you remain on guard duty until we return?"

The portly animal bristled. He raised his head toward her and snorted, pawing his front feet. She chuckled as Tusker pranced toward the freshly planted butterfly nursery and gently sniffed the leaves. He straightened and began an elaborate movement, which took him around the plant like a guard on patrol. Pausing at irregular intervals to search the area, smell the air, and check on his charges. He resumed his self-assigned dance, which Destiny imagined was a lovely musical masterpiece in his mind.

She swayed in tune, only pausing when

Valerian rested a hand on her shoulder. "I'm sorry to ask you to repeat it," he quietly murmured. "But I don't speak animal like you. What's going on?"

"Bran said we shouldn't leave the caterpillars and eggs unguarded while Soarant takes us across the savannah. The smaller birds and wrens will feast on the insects, and the precious children of Butterfly will be lost. Tusker has volunteered to guard them. He's so committed to his patrol. He says he will rejoin us once Soarant returns to protect them himself."

Valerian implored, "I am worried about Tusker rejoining us out on the savannah. We'll be across the expanse in a short morning cycle, but it will take him days. How will we find each other? I'm not fond of this plan. Don't think me stupid."

Destiny touched Valerian's cheek and

smiled. "I am glad you finally like Tusker and Bran, too."

"I want a better answer. We are a team now. We shouldn't leave anyone behind."

Bran's shiny black feathers rustled. He cawed and squealed, then bobbed his head excitedly from the top of the rock.

Destiny grinned and nodded. "You're right, Bran. Let's have Soarant take us all, including Butterfly's nursery. That way, no one is left behind, and the dragon's new family will remain safe. Come on, Bran, let's announce the change in plans."

She carefully approached the massive creature and bowed. "Soarant, we're worried about Butterfly's eggs and caterpillars while you take us across the savannah. Can you bring the hosting plants with us so the young ones aren't eaten? Do you have enough room

in the broad pouch underneath your tail for
all of us?"

Soarant extended his head so their eyes
were level and replied, "You're worried about
Butterfly's family and don't want to leave

Tusker behind to guard? Your heart is pure. Your concern is touching. It is little wonder the traveler has come to collect you. I will call out to the creatures of my forest. They will stand guard until I return. Have no fear for my Butterfly brood, Dreamer."

She gently stroked his cheek's smooth, cool scales with an even touch. "Thank you."

"Tell your companions it's time to leave. Gather them at the clearing. We will leave after I have given instructions to the new protectors."

Valerian faced Soarant and asked in a worried tone, "The traveler wants to collect my sister? What are we heading into, mighty one?"

"I see many things, young man," the dragon replied. "But, I'm only an observer. You will meet your fate soon enough. Then the rest is up to Destiny."

She beamed. "Come on." Looping her hand over her brother's arm. She joyfully added, "Let's gather for the journey. Val, can you get Tusker to join us? He would like to hear it coming from you."

He patted her hand and grumbled, "I've got to stop telling you everything that comes into my mind. I hope Tusker doesn't nuzzle me for worrying about him."

Her laughter was filled with excitement.

chapter eight

The journey took a majority of the daylight. Each traveler rode comfortably in the dragon's pouch. Soarant finally reared up, changing the angle of his wings to allow him to elegantly land light as a feather. Tusker promptly trotted away from the massive creature and relieved himself.

Valerian anxiously called, "Careful, Soarant, he sometimes pees on other's feet. Watch out." The young man took in the change in the landscape. The savannah had given way to large, rocky formations, waterfalls, and tall trees scattered here and there. The sun was bright. He felt more relaxed and calmer than on the edge of the savannah.

"Farewell and safe travels, Destiny and Valerian," called Soarant as he turned and flew into the crystal blue skies.

Both the youngsters waved and replied in unison, "Thank you for transporting us."

Bran excitedly hopped around, making a variety of sounds. While his sister followed the bird's conversation, Valerian frowned at this lack of understanding, wishing he had her ability to speak with the animals.

When Bran stopped, Tusker began bobbing up and down, wiggling his backside with great excitement. Destiny's eyes brightened as she swayed to the beat. Valerian felt sad at being left out of the conversation.

"For corn's sake, Des, what has everyone riled up?"

Bran jumped to a small metal object on the ground and retrieved it with his beak. Then, with a twist of his body and head, he tossed it to Destiny, who giggled when she snatched it in flight.

She held up the shiny, black and silver object. "Have you ever seen anything like this before?"

Valerian studied it in her hand and shook his head. "No, I haven't."

She pitched it to him.

He, too, quickly caught the object. "It's hard as a rock yet light beyond belief. No one from our village could make such a device."

"I saw it in my dream," she proudly exclaimed as she moved closer, facing him. "I told Bran to look for it. I'm so glad he found one. I dreamed that several were laid out for us to find. My dream showed that a shiny man would come once we located one and moved it."

Sensing danger, Val clutched his sister's hands, planning to pull her close as Tusker lumbered to her side and Bran lit on her shoulder. He insisted, "We need to run while we still can. Anything that can build a smooth, lightweight object like this must be dangerous. This is…witchcraft, just like what the elders warned us to avoid. We will suffer at the hands of…why are you staring at me?"

No one spoke or moved a muscle in response. He realized they were staring at something behind him. The sudden buzzes, whirls, and clicks emanating from behind paralyzed him. He struggled to turn when a hand rested on his shoulder. Instantly, his terror abated. He heard a soothing voice resonating in his mind.

Destiny's bright eyes met his as she nodded in agreement at the voice. Her brother turned around and pulled his sister close to his side with a protective arm.

"We have come a great distance in search of you, Dreamer. I do not doubt that the small female with sparkling green eyes and yellow hair is someone my people need. I'm glad I was chosen to seek you out."

"I saw you in my dream," she calmly replied. "You said I have a great challenge ahead if I accept."

The shiny being in front of them, speaking their language, was taller than any man at home.

The shiny being knelt. "Apologies, let me reduce my stature so we can speak more comfortably. Is this better?"

Valerian inclined his head, yet the uneasy sensation returned. "How can we understand one another? My sister speaks to all creatures. How do I hear you when I see no mouth and hear no sounds through my ears? You heard what I was thinking. That frightens me."

The shiny being rotated his head from side to side as if considering something. "Your sister doesn't translate languages but accepts all kinds of differences. The universe has many things you will not recognize. Trying to force those realities into something comfortable for you is useless. Your sole companion with that approach is fear and panic. Living creatures go mad trying to pigeonhole foreign things because there is no frame of reference."

Destiny squeezed his hand as she transferred a thought to her brother. "Open your mind, Val. You can do this."

chapter nine

Destiny straightened and announced aloud. "Mr. Shiny, before I respond to your challenge offer, I must know my brother's fate and the fate of our loyal companions. We have been through much. I want them in my life."

They stood attentively as the buzzes, whirls, and clicks formed a calming conversation in their minds. "You may address me as Oberon. My leaders knew you would want your companions to go on this sojourn. However, Tusker and Bran must remain here. There is however great value in keeping Valerian close for what you will soon face."

Destiny's heart was bathed in sadness regarding the creatures.

Oberon added, "Tusker and Bran are noble but belong here. Without their kind to mix with, loneliness will consume them. We will return them to their kind and erase their knowledge of you and your brother. The animals will live their days happy and content, though your heart will be heavy at them going."

Valerian protested, "We're a team. We couldn't have made it without them. I say no. If they don't go, then…"

Destiny tugged on Valerian's arm to end the discussion. Her eyes were filled with tears, and she slowly hugged and stroked their trusted companions in turn. Valerian followed suit, whispering thank you to the noble swine.

Destiny drew a ragged breath. "Tusker, Bran, we must part ways. I will see you in my dreams and watch over you. I could not bear to watch you die of loneliness because I was selfish to keep you with me. Oberon, please keep your promise to see to their wellbeing."

Valerian kicked a stone and complained, "I guess this means we accept the challenge. Let's do this so we can return home again."

Destiny whirled and confronted her brother. "Val, there's no going back to that life. I've seen our new home. Our lives will change forever. It didn't occur to me that you might not want to leave Settlefore for a new place in Oberon's world. If we go, we can't come back."

After his usual noises, Oberon interjected, "That's inaccurate. As the chosen princess, you and your brother will have the power to return to your walled city. No one would hold you against your will. However after thousands of generations of ruler selection done in this manner, no one mentally or emotionally wishes to go back."

Valerian was dumbfounded. Destiny smoothed his hair behind an ear and gently offered, "Yes, Val, I saw this coming, too. The stars we see in the night sky have homes like ours. The chosen princess is to lead everyone. I didn't tell you the whole dream because I feared you'd believe me mad." She patted his arm and stared into his eyes. "My dear brother, I wanted you with me on this adventure, so I only gave you bits and pieces. If I'm to govern the vast light sources in the sky, I need you."

Destiny sensed the anger, fear, and frustration swirling inside of him.

He looked at her as water pooled in his vibrant green eyes. "I can't honestly feel betrayed when you asked me to go along.

You're my sister whom I have watched over for years. I cannot be parted from you. Please, I need a hug to settle my emotions."

She rushed into him so hard she heard, "Oof!"

chapter ten

Valerian stepped back to wipe the tears from his eyes. He gathered his strength, hugged Tusker, and stroked Bran's beautiful silky feathers. He stared deeply into the dark eyes. "I will miss you and think often of this time of my life. Perhaps, in time, I will be able to visit you in shared dreams as the trusted companions you are. I am sad you won't remember us, but it's best that way."

Each creature produced sounds and dis-played actions until he understood what they conveyed. He choked back his sadness and smiled. He glanced at Destiny, who intently

watched the scene with smiles, chuckles, and a few tears.

Oberon's buzzes, whirls, and clicks launched. "I will take them now that farewells have been exchanged. They will be happy in their homes and remain safe from hunters. Then it will be your turn."

Valerian blinked, rubbing his eyes. Confused, he gazed around and stammered, "Where'd they go, Destiny? I stared at them, thinking about another hug, and then they vanished." He tapped his chin with one finger. "I do recall they looked like they were about to fall asleep."

"Oberon's people are masters of dream travel," she said. "He looked into their dreams and saw their homes. He activated their sleep button, and they did the rest. They dreamed of home. It's what we're going to do, dear brother."

Valerian trembled, and his eyes widened with dread. "That's not possible, Destiny." He stomped a foot on the ground and grabbed her hand. "You said you had a dream. We needed to meet Mr. Shiny, which we did. Now you're telling me he will do some magic and make me fall asleep. Then we'll wake up somewhere that isn't our home in Settlefore? Every time you tell me something, it's worse. I'm telling myself that this is all a bad dream. I'm ready to run home."

A large hand rested on Valerian's shoulder, and he froze.

The standard precursor noises occurred. "Destiny, your brother may not make the journey mentally. I sense a deep fear which will interfere with his dream travel. You must calm him or leave him for his own sake."

Destiny began to cry and pleaded, "Val, don't be afraid. I need you with me, or I can't go. It would be a cruel punishment for me to stay. Oberon's people want and need me. Don't you see, we must both go. This is the path for me."

Valerian shouted, "It's not my dream. I didn't sign up for this insanity. Please don't make me choose, Des. We've always been together, even when the guardians from Settlefore found us. We were wandering, seeking food after our village was attacked. I got us out. But our parents perished. You're my only family. Please don't leave me."

Oberon watched as Destiny reached out her hands and crossed them, stretching to her brother. "Take my hands. I will show you what you cannot see. Together, we will dream, and you will be unafraid."

Valerian sobbed as he reluctantly crossed his arms to take her hands. "Don't leave me behind. I'm so scared. I can't be left, yet I can't go."

Destiny firmly grasped his hands. She turned and nodded to Oberon before staring into Valerian's eyes. "Dream with me, my dear brother. Together, we will know of great happiness. Worrying will be a thing of the past."

Valerian struggled to stay awake.

Destiny soothed, "That's right, Val. Let the dream traveler take us to our new home."

Valerian entered the dream state and stopped shaking.

Destiny, pleased with the progress, smiled beside him.

chapter eleven

The two little girls, with long flowing blond hair and bright green eyes, shimmied into their sleeping gowns, then scampered across the floor, crawling into their large bed. Their mother followed and arranged the covers for their sleep. They were too excited.

"Momma, tell us a story," said one.

The other begged, "Tell us about when you were learning to be Dreamer."

"No, I want to hear about Uncle Valerian before he became the galaxy attorney, sitting in judgment for complaints," insisted the first.

"I want to hear about Tusker and the bobbing raven, Bran. Those stories are so much fun."

Destiny chided, tucking the noisy children under the covers. "Girls, I have to teach at the dream academy tomorrow. I need to sleep, too. Students from around the galaxy are here to learn what I teach. I do my best teaching when I have my rest." She winked, slightly grinning.

Her young daughters knew how to plead, pout, and protest enough for her to relent with a shake of her head.

Destiny began, "Once upon a time, a brother and sister lived in a land that didn't believe in dreams. Dreams were considered silly and nonsensical, not to be pursued."

The two young girls exclaimed, "Momma, how can that be? Didn't they know?"

"The brother wasn't sure about dreams, but the sister knew." She smoothed the covers, and they stilled at her touch. "She always knew that if you follow your dreams and your heart is pure, you will have great fortune."

"But, Momma, what if the dreams hurt others? What if the dreamer has a black heart?"

Destiny sternly admonished, "Those terrible dreams from a black heart are poison. No good can come from that person, and everything they touch will die. This is why we teach people to dream good things, my darling daughters. Now, it is time for sleep. Dream like I have taught you. Someday, you might take my place as a ruler."

Destiny kissed each of their foreheads, pulled the covers up, and dimmed the lights. Smiling, she quietly left the nursery for her bed and loving prince, knowing her dreams lasted forever.

Word Search The Dreamer

```
H O B U Y O W E K Z U H R P V O P F T H Q K A N
L F K U I S E N Y A K E Q R C M Z D V H X X C G
A W D E S T I N Y P T Z X I N U M R N O G A R D
Y Z D S T O A N F N R W C N F G P Y J Y S N F I
N I I H I Q T L U H E N K C R U E J S A J B W X
M O I C E B E H F B M I S E S G A Z V T R M I J
P B R N P B L A B W A B A S Y E F Z T A I U J J
M S L E S X G I E B E Q C S J X X I V E U C C T
T T J U B U L R N D R E K N C R U E Q L F M A H
M R I W R O U K U G D R V Q P L Y H W U N S G L
B Z A Q L T E I X T S N A S O G O L L N Y K S H
D C I V N B Z R R N O U L Z G U U U M H L E U U
W K V E E T E A V I U O E Q I G I Z D P F N V S
Z C V I V N E X J K X G R N B E T Y K C C S K F
Y D F I T H R H E C R U I T V R Z S P C I B Z W
A X V L G A V C D S G U I Y N E Q I S P L T W S
T B J B E U R E A B C H A L L E N G E V K T Y V
L U R F F N A W W W P S N F M U O N U B R A N R
F A C E S Y E R P E R J C R O G K G Z I F L T P
P W C R P N J R D T I S D E T U S K E R M R P K
N Z Q K P O E D K I U U C T P F U E C T P F T R
A G W D F O U S W C A J P T N J S G U J O J X Z
S M F Y V F T H C D O N R U C M Y A S T P P V F
Z X G U W V W S A A P L S B M X L O J M E O Z F
```

Challenge	Princess	Heart	Adventure
Butterfly	Fear	Brave	Siblings
Mystical	Dreamer	CloudCity	Bran
Destiny	Valeriian	Oberon	Raven
Tusker	Hunter	Guardian	Dragon

Answer Matching

1. What is Cloud City?

2. What does the guardian wait for?

3. What is Destiny's special gift?

4. Why does Valerian go on this adventure?

5. What is Soarant's special skill?

6. What is Bran's skill?

7. How does Oberon transport the characters

8. What is Tusker's value to the journey?

9. What is the guardian saved from?

10. What did the hunter do?

A. Protection

B. Loneliness

C. Butterfly

D. Shot the arrow

E. Dreams

F. Where the adventure starts

G. Finder of resources

H. Strength and honor

I. Crossing the savannah

J. Accepts all differences

Parents: The answer keys are available for download from our website *EnigmaSeries.com* under the free tab.

Knowledge Check

Across

2. Who demands his arrow be returned?

5. Who is afraid to go to sleep?

6. Soarant waits for whom?

9. Who do the adventurers save?

10. What is the guardian?

Down

1. The hero in The Dreamer

3. What place did the adventurers leave?

4. What is Bran?

7. What is Mr. Shiny's name

8. How do the adventures reach their destination?

Parents: The answer keys are available for download from our website *EnigmaSeries.com* under the free tab.

Word Scramble The Dreamer

1. ARDNIGAU _______________________________

2. IDETSNY _______________________________

3. NRTOASA _______________________________

4. VALENIRA _______________________________

5. BEORON _______________________________

6. ETURSK _______________________________

7. AYLCSMIT _______________________________

8. ANRB _______________________________

9. CULOD YITC _______________________________

10. EAMERRD _______________________________

About the Authors Rox & Charles

Rox Burkey is the COO of Enigma Series, LLC, and uses her extensive professional knowledge of optimizing technology and business investments to drive stellar customer experiences into the ongoing stories of Enigma Series. Characteristics of people she has met over her career are woven into their stories. Rox enjoys her family, friends, puppies, reading, reviewing books, and traveling whenever possible. Meeting readers at various events is one of her favorite pastimes.

Charles Breakfield is the CTO of Enigma Series, LLC, and he leverages his decades of technology expertise, including security, networking, voice, and anything digital, to bring innovative technothriller elements into storytelling. He has a deep knowledge of World War II history, has traveled extensively, and seeks cultural exchanges to learn what makes different people tick. Charles enjoys wine tasting, wine-making, Harley riding, cooking new recipes and extravaganzas, and woodworking.

We wrote this fantasy, dedicated to ages 14 and above, to encourage young readers to be creative and dream. If you are reading the ePUB please visit our website and download the coloring pages.

Happy imagination.

www.ingramcontent.com/pod-product-compliance
Lightning Source LLC
Chambersburg PA
CBHW040231170726
48295CB00014B/885